RAYA AND THE LAST DRAGON

RAYA'S WORLD

written by
Julia March

Contents

Long ago, Kumandra was a united world where humans and dragons lived in peace.

Then people began to fight. This attracted dark beings called the Druun who turned everyone to stone.

The dragons sacrificed themselves and used their magic to drive the Druun away.

Today, Kumandra is divided. Just one piece of dragon power remains. Could it be the key to fixing this broken world?

Fang
A thriving, wealthy land where people love gold and cats

Spine
A remote, mountainous land famed for its fierce warriors

Heart
A peaceful, prosperous land with a perfectly circular natural island

Talon
A bustling port and crossroads for travellers and traders

Kumandra

Even though the last dragon chased away the Druun, peace did not return to Kumandra. The people remained angry and suspicious of each other. Today, Kumandra is split into five rival lands: Fang, Heart, Spine, Talon, and Tail. The only thing that unites them is the mighty Dragon River.

Tail
A desert land of scattered settlements and tough people

Heart

This lush, prosperous land holds something very special – the mystical Dragon Gem. The dragons entrusted it to Heart centuries ago. It has been kept safe in the Dragon Temple ever since. Heart's chief, Benja, is a Guardian of the Dragon Gem. He watches over his people and his daughter, Raya.

Bridge from Heart to the other lands

Young Raya

Raya lives in Heart and grew up listening to stories about dragons. She has always longed to become a Guardian of the Dragon Gem, like her father, Chief Benja. He challenges her to reach the gem's hiding place in the Dragon Temple!

Baby Tuk Tuk

Tuk Tuk is Raya's loyal pet. He is just a baby, small enough to be carried in a bag.

Brave and bold

When Raya is 12 years old, she thinks she is ready to become a Guardian of the Dragon Gem. She will have to prove to her father that she is ready for the task.

Sneaky steps

Sneaking into the temple is tricky! Tuk Tuk helps by rolling past a row of booby traps, setting them off.

A warrior's trial

Benja does not go easy on Raya. Her skills in stealth, agility, and sword fighting must be tested.

Guardian ceremony

Raya passes the test, and Benja pours sacred water over her. The droplets glow like the Dragon Gem itself. Raya is now a guardian!

The Dragon Gem

Deep within the Dragon Temple is a hidden chamber. Here floats the legendary Dragon Gem. It is said that the last dragon, Sisu, used the gem to chase away the Druun. This glowing orb contains the only dragon powers left in Kumandra. No wonder the Guardians of the Gem protect it so fiercely!

A pond surrounds the floating gem

The gem draws water to it

Benja

Loving father, leader, peacemaker

Raya's father, Chief Benja, rules the land of Heart. He is a man with a plan: to make Kumandra one big, happy world again. However, although he is a man of peace, Benja is no pushover. His sword-fighting skills have earned him the nickname "the baddest blade in the five lands".

Things you need to know about Benja:

1 – His beloved daughter, Raya, calls Benja "ba".

2 – Benja has built a bridge to join Heart to the other lands.

3 – He believes the world is broken because people don't trust each other.

4 – Benja is a really great chef!

Broken world

Benja's bridge between Heart and the other lands is completed. It is time to welcome the people of Fang, Talon, Tail, and Spine. Raya notices how the four groups stand apart, afraid to mix together. Is her father's gesture of friendship all in vain? Can this broken world be mended?

Betrayal

When the clans visit, Raya quickly befriends the young Fang princess, Namaari. They both love dragons! Namaari shares a secret – Fang has an old scroll that tells of the last dragon in Kumandra. Raya decides to share a secret of her own...

Friendly welcome

Benja encourages Raya to give the visitors a warm welcome, setting aside any rumours she may have heard about them.

A secret shared

Raya leads her new friend into the Dragon Temple. Namaari gazes in awe at the glowing Dragon Gem!

Namaari's trap

Namaari summons the Fang soldiers, who are followed by the other guests. They all fight over the gem. Even Benja cannot stop them.

Druun attack!

The gem is dropped and breaks into five shards. Then the Druun attack! Each clan grabs a shard – then flees.

One last hope

Benja's leg is hurt and he cannot run. He has just a moment to hand his gem shard to Raya before the Druun turn him to stone. While there is light in the gem, there is still hope.

Benja pushes Raya to safety before being turned to stone

Escape!

The fighting attracted the Druun, just like it did centuries ago. These smokelike beings thrive on conflict, and multiply by passing through victims and turning them to stone. Benja uses all his strength to save Raya from them. He pushes her into the river, and she is carried away by the flow.

Raya

Brave warrior

It has been six years since Raya shared the location of the Dragon Gem and disaster struck. She is now searching for a dragon hero who she believes can help her. Raya is clever and funny, but Tuk Tuk is her only friend. As she travels across Kumandra, she meets many new people – but can she trust them?

Things you need to know about Raya:

1 – Raya is the daughter of Benja, chief of the land of Heart.

2 – Raya wants to fix the Dragon Gem and save Kumandra.

3 – She is a daring sword fighter who has learned to survive on her own.

4 – She finds it hard to trust people in case they betray her.

23

Raya's quest

Raya's determination to find the dragon never falters. If she succeeds, her beloved father – and other Kumandrans turned to stone by the Druun – might live again.

The last dragon was not turned to stone like the others. She must still be out there! Surely that dragon can save Kumandra again – if only Raya can find her.

Find the dragon

Raya knows that Namaari is tracking her across Kumandra. She must give Namaari the slip, or she will certainly interfere with Raya's plans.

Avoid Namaari

The other lands each have a shard of the Dragon Gem. Raya must visit all four lands to collect the shards, add them to her own, and return the gem to one piece.

Restore the gem

With the gem fixed, the dragon will be able to "boom" away the Druun and stone people will return to life. Perhaps Benja's dream of a united Kumandra can even come true.

Destroy the Druun

Tuk Tuk

Ready to roll

Is it a woodlouse? An armadillo? No, it's Tuk Tuk! This giant but gentle creature is more than Raya's pet – he is her best friend and faithful steed. Tuk Tuk is a slow walker, but he can move very quickly when he rolls up into a wheel shape! Raya just has to hop aboard and point him in the right direction.

Things you need to know about Tuk Tuk:

1 – Tuk Tuk joins Raya on her quest to find the last dragon.

2 – He can be stubborn, but food usually wins him over.

3 – When he was a baby, Tuk Tuk was so small that he could sit on Raya's shoulder.

4 – He sometimes rolls over onto his back if he is startled.

Long cloak with raw silk lining

Woven, broad-brimmed hat

Comfortable saddle with secure handholds

Tough, armoured skin protects Tuk Tuk when he rolls

Bold traveller

Raya is equipped to deal with anything she might face on her journey. Her cloak shields her from the elements. She carries a satchel close to her body, which holds the gem shard, food, money, and a map. Raya's travelling buddy, Tuk Tuk, carries a bedroll and Raya's sword on the back of his saddle.

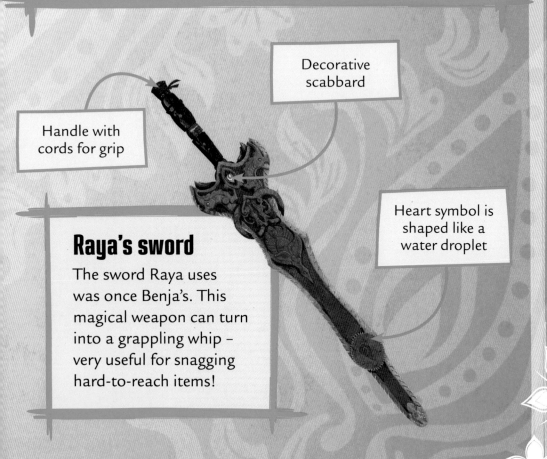

Decorative scabbard

Handle with cords for grip

Heart symbol is shaped like a water droplet

Raya's sword

The sword Raya uses was once Benja's. This magical weapon can turn into a grappling whip – very useful for snagging hard-to-reach items!

Tail

Far to the east of Kumandra lies Tail. This parched desert land grows drier by the year as the waters slowly recede. Its once busy dock is now a ghost town. The people of Tail live in scattered settlements. They are hardy folk who survive by reusing and recycling. Nothing goes to waste in Tail!

Raya follows a trickle of water into an old shipwreck

Thickly braided hair

The long search

Raya is searching for Sisu, Kumandra's last dragon. An ancient scroll says Sisu is asleep "at the river's end", but the river has many branches, each ending in a different place. One by one, Raya tries them all until there is just one left, in distant Tail. If Sisu is not there, exhausted Raya will have to give up.

Namaari

Friend or foe?

Young Namaari met Raya when the Fang people visited Heart and the two became friends. But Namaari betrayed Raya, and her actions left the Dragon Gem in shards. Now fully grown, she is a fierce warrior who believes Raya is her enemy. Namaari vows to stop Raya from finding the last dragon.

Things you need to know about Namaari:

1 — Namaari's mother is Virana, chief of the land of Fang.

2 — She has a brilliant mind but can be sneaky and calculating.

3 — Namaari is a hero in her land. She will do anything, and fight anyone, to protect Fang.

4 — She truly loves dragons – just as much as Raya does.

Fang

Fang is situated at the head of the Dragon River. This thriving land is known for its proud royal family, its angular buildings, and its unfriendliness towards outsiders. The cat-loving Fang people have dug a canal around their main city to keep others out. They are all about power – not sharing!

Land is now an artificial island

Cerlots

Giant cats called Cerlots are native to Fang. These agile beasts are trained as mounts for Fang's fierce warriors.

Fang Palace, home to Namaari and Chief Virana

Fang island forms an eye in the river's head

Steps leading to raised Fang City buildings

Uncertain Raya can only hope Sisu wakes up

Sticky rice cakes float away on the water

Waking Sisu

Raya finds the last dragon's sleeping place in an old shipwreck on the edge of Tail. But how do you wake a sleeping dragon? Raya sets down an offering of incense and rice to lure Sisu out. It works – although Sisu points out that it is a small serving for a hungry dragon!

Sisu is excited to meet Raya – and to eat!

Dragon powers

The magic in the Dragon Gem belonged to Sisu's brothers and sisters. As Raya and Sisu find the missing gem shards, Sisu gains her family's dragon powers one by one.

A glowing dragon is an amazing sight. When Sisu uses her little sister Amba's glow power, her eyes light up and she shines and shimmers like a beautiful blue star.

Glow power

Shape-shifting

Sisu's sister Pranee could disguise herself as a human! When Sisu uses the shape-shifting power, she turns into a young woman with long, purple hair.

Sometimes a dragon does not want to be seen. Sisu uses her brother Jagan's fog power to cloak herself in a thick mist, which is impossible to see through.

Fog disguise

Rain creation

Rain creation was the power of Sisu's big brother Pengudatu. It allows Sisu to summon rain at will and then fly across the sky by running on the raindrops.

Sisu

Shape-shifter supreme

When Raya retrieves a new gem shard, Sisu the dragon gains an important power. It is the power to shape-shift into human form. Sisu is just as optimistic and trusting in her human form as she is as a dragon. She is just as hungry, too. Well, who wouldn't be after 500 years of sleep?

Things you need to know about Sisu:

1 — The name Sisu is short for Sisudatu.

2 — Her long, purple hair looks like her dragon form's mane.

3 — Raya has to keep warning Sisu not to reveal her dragon form to strangers.

4 — In human form, Sisu never walks in a straight line.

Boun

Tough business boy

Boun grew up by himself on the streets of a remote Tail port after losing his parents to the Druun. This tough little cookie is making his way in the world on his own terms. Still only 10, Boun already runs his own restaurant – the result of hard work, shrewd business sense, and just a little hustling!

Things you need to know about Boun:

1 – Boun owns and runs a floating shrimp restaurant.

2 – He is upset when Raya suggests his congee might be poisoned.

3 – His greatest wish is to earn plenty of jade – the currency of Kumandra.

4 – Boun can sometimes feel scared and alone.

Talon

Talon's port is at the centre of the Dragon River and is an important crossroads for travellers. Goods arrive on battered boats at ramshackle piers, before being bought and sold at a bustling market. Merchants (and con artists) can make lots of jade on these busy streets.

Brightly coloured market stalls

47

The Ongis

Here, there, and everywhere

The Ongis have one aim – to rob unwary visitors to the port of Talon. Distraction tactics are their speciality. Uka, Pan, and Dyan descend like a whirlwind. The Ongis confuse and bamboozle victims so they do not notice their bags being emptied. No one, not even Raya, is ready for the Ongis.

Things you need to know about the Ongis:

1 — Their names also mean one, two, and three.

2 — They operate as a team and are never far apart.

3 — They work with a toddler named Noi to help distract passers-by.

4 — They will steal anything – even pieces of Dragon Gem!

Know your Ongis

The Ongis are Uka, Pan, and Dyan. Uka means "one", Pan means "two", and Dyan means "three". Telling them apart is as easy as one, two, three as well! Read about their features, then match the numbered pictures to the Ongis below.

Dyan
- Has a topknot
- Wears a wide hat
- Often looks very grumpy

Pan
- Is the plumpest
- Has a wide smile
- Wears a cone-shaped hat

Uka
- Has big eyes
- Has only four whiskers
- Is very small

Noi

Little Noi, big trouble

Aww... isn't she sweet? This tiny tot from Talon doesn't look like a troublemaker. In fact, she just never gets caught! Noi is a hustler who commands the Ongis with a snap of her fingers. Noi distracts passers-by with happy gurgles or fake tears while the sneaky Ongis steal from them.

Things you need to know about Noi:

1 — Noi has been a hustler all her life (that's two years).

2 — Noi pronounces Sisu's name as "Soo soo".

3 — Noi's distraction skills help get Raya past the bodyguards at the Talon chief's house.

4 — She wears her short hair in six small knots.

Sisu in human form is bundled onto Tuk Tuk

Trouble in Talon

In search of another gem piece, Raya and Sisu both go looking for Dang Hai, the Talon chief. Instead, they meet his mother, Dang Hu. This elderly lady looks sweet, but she is really very tough. She tries to trick Sisu, but Raya charges to the rescue on Tuk Tuk, grabbing the gem shard as she goes!

Raya swipes Talon's shard

Mammoth tusks on chief's house

Spine

The land of Spine sits high in the snowy, bamboo-covered mountains. This remote place is said to be home to giant, angry warriors. Even from afar, travellers can see the spiked walls of the Spine fortress and hear war drums beating. The mighty noise suggests a mighty force lives inside!

Bamboo cabins

Spiked entrance
to the fortress

Bridge over
deep ravine

Tong

One-man land

Tong is the only person left in Spine. Everyone else moved away to seek a better life! It has been years since Tong has done any fighting, but he still looks every inch a warrior. Tong bonds with Raya and her new friends, especially tiny but tough Noi. The cute toddler brings out Tong's protective side.

Things you need to know about Tong:

1 – Tong wears Spine's gem shard on a necklace.

2 – These days, Tong mainly uses his axe for chopping vegetables.

3 – He has a set of wind chimes that sound like an army playing multiple war drums.

4 – Tong always hoped the other Spine people would return.

Sisu is now missing just one dragon power

Trusting people is a new experience for Raya

Open fire gives a merry crackle

60

Coming together

Thanks to Tong, Raya's gang now has four out of five gem shards. To celebrate, they share a meal – and their dreams of a united Kumandra, free from the Druun. To bring their dreams to life, they must restore the gem, but Fang holds the final piece of the puzzle...

Soup is a tasty combination of ingredients from their lands

Hope and doubt

Namaari has the final shard of the Dragon Gem – the key to saving Kumandra. Will she give it up? Sisu trusts Namaari will help them. Raya thinks they might have to fight her!

Sisu

I know a true dragon fan when I see one. Just look at her eyes, all misty...

Namaari is acting all mean and tough, but I can sense the good in her heart.

If you want someone's trust, you have to give a little trust first.

Raya

Namaari betrayed me before. I won't let her do it again. Once bitten, twice shy!

Look – she's got a crossbow! She's going to hurt Sisu, and the Druun will never be defeated.

Maybe it's not too late to end this peacefully. That's what my father would want.

Penguin Random House

Project Editor Beth Davies
Senior Designer Lauren Adams
Managing Editor Paula Regan
Managing Art Editor Jo Connor
Production Editor Siu Yin Chan
Senior Production Controller Lloyd Robertson
Publisher Julie Ferris
Art Director Lisa Lanzarini
Publishing Director Mark Searle

DK would like to thank Chelsea Alon and Rima Simonian at Disney for their assistance; and Jennette ElNaggar at DK for proofreading.

First published in Great Britain in 2021 by Dorling Kindersley Limited One Embassy Gardens, 8 Viaduct Gardens, London SW11 7BW A Penguin Random House Company

10 9 8 7 6 5 4 3 2 1
001–318591–Feb/2021

PILL 07-05-21

PILLGWENLLY

A CIP catalogue record for this book is available from the British Library.

ISBN 978-0-24143-920-3

Printed in China

For the curious
www.dk.com